Bees like Flc

Rebecca Bielawski

www.booksbeck.com

Bees like flowers,
Look!   A buzzy bee!
Sometimes they sting people,
But they never sting me.

You see,

she's got a fluffy body,
But, don't touch her
'cause she might...

Get you with her stinger,
As you've given her a fright.

I don't bother them – they're working,
I just watch them do their thing.

They walk around on flowers,
And stick their little faces in.

Bees like flowers,
That are growing in the ground.

Bright colours bring them closer,
And keep them buzzing round.

Bees like flowers,

And the nectar
that's so sweet.

But,
when they fly away,
Something sticks on
to their feet.

It's pollen and it's yellow,
Look, it's sticking to the bee.

She takes it to another flower,

Or the blossoms
of a tree.

So, flowers like
bees too,

"Thank you bees,"
they say.

They help to spread the pollen,
And make new flowers far away.

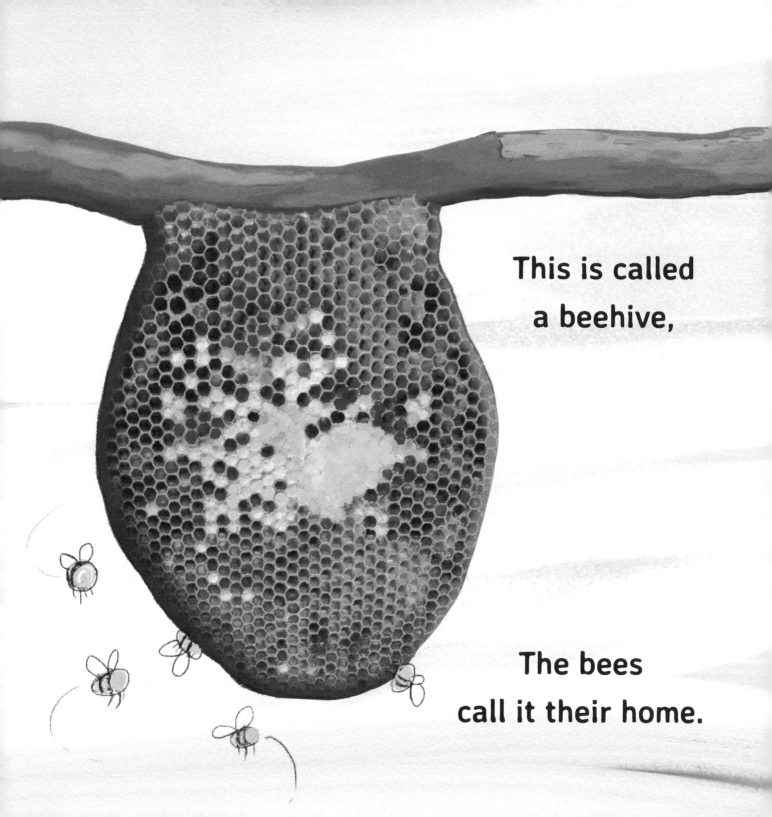

This is called
a beehive,

The bees
call it their home.

The queen lays her eggs in there,
Inside the honeycomb.

Bees use the nectar,
To make honey in the hive,

They feed it to the babies,
When they finally arrive.

Yummy, runny honey,
made by our friends
the bees,

They might give you a little bit...

If you would just say,
"please".

So, that's why bees like flowers,
And that's why...

The End

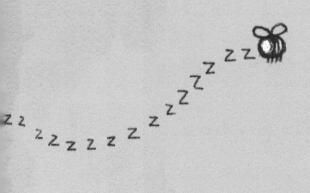

Insect Bodies

Insects have 6 legs.
Count my legs.

Insects have 3 parts to their bodies.
Count my body parts.

Am I an **insect?**

Flower Names

Poppy

Sunflower

Daisy

Can you find them in the story?

MUMMY NATURE
SERIES

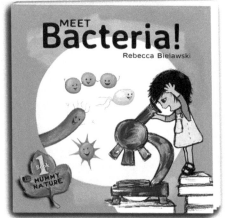

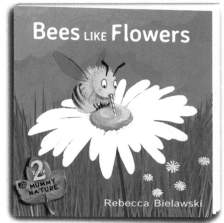

More children's books

See preview pages, FREE printables, book planning sketches and author articles
Stay up to date on book promos and new releases by Rebecca Bielawski
Ebooks and print books in English and Spanish

www.booksbeck.com

CPSIA information can be obtained
at www.ICGtesting.com
Printed in the USA
BVHW022334310122
627724BV00002B/17